"Who wants to watch T[...]
Henrietta's mother after [...]
tonight."

"ME!" shouted Daniel and Henrietta together.
They weren't usually allowed to watch television
in the evening. But tonight Mother had decided to
give the[...]

"Well i[...]
finish y[...]
and h[...]
t[...]

HENRIETTA'S
BUBBLE TROUBLE

Starring Henrietta:

HENRIETTA'S BUBBLE TROUBLE

Stan Cullimore

Illustrated by John Farman

YOUNG CORGI BOOKS

HENRIETTA'S BUBBLE TROUBLE

A YOUNG CORGI BOOK 0 552 52746 7

First publication in Great Britain by Piccadilly Press Ltd.

PRINTING HISTORY
Piccadilly Press edition published 1991
Young Corgi edition published 1993

Young Corgi Books are published by Transworld Publishers Ltd.,
61–63 Uxbridge Road, Ealing, London W5 5SA, in Australia by
Transworld Publishers (Australia) Pty. Ltd., 15–25 Helles Avenue,
Moorebank, NSW 2170, and in New Zealand by Transworld Publishers
(N.Z.) Ltd., 3 William Pickering Drive, Albany, Auckland.

Printed and bound in Great Britain by
Cox & Wyman Ltd., Reading, Berkshire

CONTENTS

CONTENTS

STORY ONE

BUBBLE TROUBLE

"Who wants to watch Top Of The Pops?" asked Henrietta's mother after tea one day. "It's on tonight."

"ME!" shouted Daniel and Henrietta together. They weren't usually allowed to watch television in the evening. But tonight Mother had decided to give them a special treat.

"We love Top Of The Pops," they cried.

"Well in that case, you, young man,

had better finish your homework. And you, young lady, go and have your bath. Hurry up though, it's on in ten minutes."

"Can I have bubbles, Mum? Please!"

Henrietta's mother stopped feeding Baby-Rose and turned to look at Henrietta.

"If you promise not to make a mess like you did last time, yes, you can have bubbles."

"Thanks, Mum. I'll be careful, honest I will." Henrietta ran up the stairs and into the bathroom.

"Chance would be a fine thing," muttered her mother.

Daniel looked up. "Henrietta can't have a bath without making a mess. It's impossible!"

He sighed, his most sensible sigh. "Not like me, I even wipe the bathtub when I'm finished, don't I, Mummy?"

His mother nodded. "Yes, Daniel. We

all know how tidy you are. I just wish
Henrietta could learn something from
you!"

She thought for a moment.

"That gives me an idea." She sat down.
"Can you run upstairs and tell Henrietta
that I'm going to come and check the
bathroom when she's finished with it. And
if it isn't totally tidy, she won't be

watching Top Of The Pops when it comes on!"

Daniel grinned. "Great. Then I won't have to put up with her singing along to all the records." He pulled a face. "I hate it when she sings. She sounds like a cat with a sore throat! I hope she's really messy tonight."

"Now that's not a very nice thing to say," said his mother. "Anyway, you run along and tell Henrietta what I said then you can come and finish your homework."

"I've finished it already," replied Daniel. He picked up his notebook and hurried into the hallway.

Upstairs in the bath Henrietta was covered all over in soft frothy bubbles. So was the floor.

"Yippee," she cried, as she pushed her rubber duck under the water. "I love bubbles." She picked up a handful and

blew them into the air. They landed on the windowsill. There was a knock at the door.

"Come in," shouted Henrietta.

It was Daniel.

"Hello, Henrietta, having fun?"

Henrietta sat up and frowned at Daniel. "That is the *stupidest* question

I've ever heard. Of course I'm having fun. What does it look like?"

"It looks like you're making a mess. There are toys all over the place, you've got bubbles on the windowsill," he shuddered, "and you haven't bothered to put the top back on the bubble bath!"

He leant over, grabbed the bottle and quickly screwed the lid back on. Then he placed it back on the shelf, in its usual place.

Henrietta laughed.

"You're so fussy, Daniel."

"No I'm not. I just hate it when you leave everything lying around. I like things to be tidy!"

Henrietta yawned.

"You're so boring, Daniel. Why don't you go away and leave me alone? I haven't finished making a mess yet."

She picked up another handful of bubbles and blew them across the room.

Then she picked up her rubber duck and dropped it on the floor at Daniel's feet.

Daniel smiled. "I've got a message for you from Mum."

Henrietta wiped bubbles onto the end of her nose and lay down in the bath.

"What is it?"

Daniel grinned. "She's going to come and check the bathroom when you've finished with it."

"What!" cried Henrietta. She sat up with a SPLASH and all the bubbles flew off her nose, landing in a heap on the floor.

Daniel nodded. "There's more. If it isn't *completely* tidy –" he paused, "– then you won't be allowed to watch Top Of The Pops tonight."

Henrietta squawked and leapt out of the bath. She threw on her dressing gown and glared at Daniel.

"Why didn't you tell me as soon as you

came in the room?"

Daniel laughed. "Because I don't *want* you to watch Top Of The Pops. You always sing along and ruin it for everyone else. Anyway, it serves you right for being so untidy."

He patted the notebook he was holding. "But, since I've finished my homework *and* I never make a mess *ever*, I get to watch television."

He turned towards the door.

"MUM! You should see what

Henrietta's done in the bathroom!"

Henrietta gasped.

"You snitch." She shook her head. "You really are a creep, aren't you, Daniel!"

Daniel smiled his creepiest smile and nodded.

Just then, Henrietta heard her mother coming up the stairs.

"If you've made a mess, young lady, you're in trouble."

"Ratburgers," wailed Henrietta.

"What am I going to do?" She wrinkled her nose. "It's not, ah . . . fair, ah . . . Oh no! Not my sneezy nose."

She snatched Daniel's notebook and tried to use it as a handkerchief.

But it was too late.

"ATISHOO." She did a Henrietta hyper-sneeze that blew all the toys and bubbles into the air.

*   *   *

"I don't believe it!" cried Daniel as Mum opened the door.

The hyper-sneeze had blown all the toys into a neat pile in a corner. And all the bubbles had fallen back into the bath.

"Nor do I. Well done, Henrietta," said her mother. "You didn't make any mess at all. Off you go then, Top Of The Pops is just starting. And you, Daniel. You've finished your homework, haven't you? What on earth's the matter, Daniel?"

For a moment, Daniel did not reply. Instead he held up a soggy lump of paper.

"My homework. It's ruined. It must have fallen in the water."

"You shouldn't have brought it into the bathroom, should you?" His mother shook her head.

Henrietta sniggered.

"It serves you right doesn't it, snitch." She dug him in the ribs as she marched out.

"It was you," cried Daniel. "You made a mess all over the floor and then you sneezed on my notebook." He stamped his foot. "That's not fair!"

But no-one heard him.

Henrietta had already started to sing at the top of her voice as she jumped down the stairs, two at a time.

STORY TWO

THE LOST KEYS

"There we are," said Henrietta's mother proudly as she lifted a freshly baked fruit-cake out of the oven. "If I do say so myself, it's perfect!"

She smiled and sat the cake down on a cooling tray on the table. "I do like baking cakes," she sighed.

Henrietta ran into the room. She sniffed and her eyes widened as she breathed in the delicious aroma of warm fruit-cake.

"Mmmm! It smells scrumptious, Mum." She licked her lips and began picking up the crumbs that had fallen onto the tray.

"Can I have some?" she asked.

Her mother wagged a finger under Henrietta's nose. "No you can't. I'm saving it for tomorrow. Your friend Lucy is coming round for tea. So you can just wait until then."

Henrietta groaned. "But I'm starving, Mum."

"You can't be," cried her mother, "you've only just finished eating your dinner ten minutes ago!"

Before Henrietta could reply, her father strolled into the room.

"What a lovely smell." He looked at the cake on the table and rubbed his hands together. "Can I have some?"

"No, you can't!" Henrietta's mother shook her head. "You're as bad as Henrietta. I'm saving that cake for tomorrow, now off you go, the pair of you."

At that moment Henrietta's sensible brother Daniel marched through the door carrying the latest copy of *Computer World*. He noticed the fruit-cake on its cooling tray.

"Wow! Fruit-cake. Can I have some,

Mum? Please!"

Mother stared at him. "Daniel, I never thought I would have to say this to you, but you're as bad as your sister. Get out of my kitchen, the lot of you. Go on!"

Father burst out laughing. "Come on, you two. I think we had better leave poor Mum in peace. She's had enough of us. You can come with me to the supermarket. I've got to get all the groceries we need for the next month."

He grinned. "I'll never be able to push the trolley round all by myself. You go and fetch your coats while I get the car out."

*   *   *

Five minutes later Father walked back into the room, followed by Daniel and Henrietta wearing their coats.

"I can't find the car keys," he muttered. "Has anyone seen them recently?"

Henrietta's mother gave him a not-again look, thought for a moment and then nodded.

"Yes I have. Now where were they?"

She frowned. "Baby-Rose was playing with something. I'll bet it was your keys."

Father groaned. "That means they could be anywhere." He sighed. "There's

only one thing for it. We have to search the house from top to bottom, until we find those keys. We can't go to the supermarket without the car and we *need* those groceries!"

They split up and began searching.

Daniel went up to the bedrooms and looked carefully under all the beds.

Father began hunting round the living room.

Mother emptied the cupboard under the stairs and searched all the places where Baby-Rose liked to play.

Henrietta stayed in the kitchen and crawled round on her hands and knees, searching for the lost keys.

Baby-Rose sat in the middle of the hall and gurgled happily.

*   *   *

After a while, Henrietta sat up and scratched her head.

"Well, they aren't here," she muttered.

She heard Daniel come running down the stairs.

"They aren't up there," he shouted, as he shot into the living room.

Henrietta pulled a face. "Ratburgers! We'll never find them."

She stood up and looked at the fruit-cake still sitting on its cooling tray.

She rubbed her tummy.

"All that crawling around has made me *really* hungry." She licked her lips.

"I'm sure Mum wouldn't mind if I just had a tiny nibble . . ."

She broke off a large piece of cake and stuffed it into her mouth.

"Mmmm," she sighed.

Just then, she heard someone coming along the hall.

She shot under the table and began looking for the lost car keys.

"I can't find them," said her mother. "Can you, Henrietta?"

Henrietta shook her head. She couldn't talk because she had a mouth full of cake.

"Well, I'm going into the living room to help your father. Come and tell us if you find them, won't you?" Henrietta nodded as her mother strode off.

Quickly she swallowed her piece of cake and stood up.

"That was delicious," she sighed.

She looked round to make sure no-one else was there, then carefully broke off another even larger piece of cake. She placed it in her mouth and began to chew.

It tasted even nicer than the first piece.

Just then, the living room door opened and her father poked his head out into the hallway.

"Have you finished in the kitchen yet?" he called.

Henrietta shook her head. She couldn't

talk because her mouth was full of cake again.

"When you have, can you go and look in the bathroom?" he continued.

Henrietta nodded as her father's head disappeared back into the front room. She gulped down the piece of cake she was eating and sat down at the table.

"That really is the nicest cake I've ever tasted," she whispered. "I'm sure Mum wouldn't mind if I just had a little bit more."

She lifted the cake off the cooling tray with both hands and opened her mouth as wide as she could.

Just then she heard footsteps, coming towards her.

She tried to put the cake back on the cooling tray. But it was too late.

So she dumped it on the table instead.

"Look!" screamed Daniel.

"Henrietta," shouted her mother.

"I might have known. Trust you, Henrietta," cried her father.

Henrietta went bright red from her toes to the tip of her nose.

"I didn't think you would mind," she stammered.

"Mind!" shouted her father. "Of course we don't mind. You're a genius! What a brilliant place to look – under the cake."

He pointed.

There, beneath the cooling tray, lying on the table and shining in the light, were the lost car keys.

"Baby-Rose must have pushed them under there," cried Mum, "and clever old Henrietta found them." She kissed Henrietta on the nose and laughed.

"I must think of a special reward for you. Now, what would you like, something to eat?"

Henrietta's father suddenly squawked and pointed to what was left of the fruit-cake on the table.

"I think that young lady's had enough to eat already. Look!"

Henrietta's mother gasped. "How could you, Henrietta! You knew I was saving that cake for tomorrow's tea. You greedy little girl!"

"She did find the keys though, didn't she?" piped Daniel.

Mother and Father exchanged glances.

"Well, yes, she did," said Mother.

"So, you should be grateful to her really, shouldn't you?" He winked at Henrietta.

Father nodded. "I suppose so."

"Of course you should!" Daniel smiled. "I've got an idea. Why don't we eat the rest of the cake now. And buy something for tomorrow's tea at the supermarket. That would be fair, wouldn't it?"

Mother and Father nodded.

Quickly Daniel ran to fetch a knife and some plates.

"Thanks, Daniel," whispered Henrietta ten minutes later as they sat in the back of the car. "You saved my life!"

Daniel shrugged his shoulders. "Not really."

"What do you mean?"

Daniel grinned. "I knew if you were left alone with that cake you wouldn't be able to stop yourself from scoffing half of it. And I *knew* that I could talk Mum and Dad into letting us eat the rest of it once you'd started it."

Henrietta snorted. "I suppose you knew the keys were hidden underneath it as well, didn't you!"

Daniel nodded.

"How?" asked Henrietta.

"Easy," whispered Daniel. "It wasn't Baby-Rose that hid the car keys at all."

He winked.

"It was *me*."

"Wow," sighed Henrietta. "Brothers do have their uses after all."

STORY THREE

THE ROLLER-SKATE RACE

One morning, during breakfast, the doorbell rang.

"I'll get it," shouted Daniel throwing down his copy of *Computer World*.

He leapt up from the table and was about to run along the hall, when he tripped over Henrietta's outstretched foot.

"AAARGH," he cried as he fell flat on his face.

Henrietta sighed. "Well if you're going

to lie on the floor all day, Daniel, I suppose I had better answer the door."

She shook her head. "You're not bad, as brothers go, Daniel. But I wish you weren't so lazy!"

Before Daniel could reply she had run down the hall and pulled open the front door.

"That's funny!" Henrietta scratched her head. "There's no-one here." She watched a large red Post Office van drive off along the road.

"Who is it, Henrietta?" called her mother.

Henrietta shrugged her shoulders. "I don't know."

Then she noticed a huge brown parcel sitting on the doorstep. It was tied up with thick orange string and one side was almost entirely covered by an enormous bright yellow stamp.

"Wow! It must have been the

postman." Henrietta stared at the stamp. "That's fantastic."

"What is it?" called her father.

"It's a parcel. Come on, Daniel, you lazybones. You can help me carry it. It's gigantic."

Puffing and panting Daniel carried the parcel into the kitchen. Henrietta was too busy getting excited to be any help.

Daniel put the parcel on the floor and stood back while Dad read the label on the top.

"It's from your Uncle Tom. He's in America at the moment. Get the scissors and we'll see what it is."

Daniel ran to fetch the scissors while Henrietta stared at the beautiful yellow stamp. It was the biggest and prettiest stamp she had ever seen.

Dad snipped the string and unwrapped the brown paper. Inside the parcel were three boxes. One for Daniel, one for

Henrietta and one for Baby-Rose. There was also a letter addressed to their parents.

Her mother picked it up and read it out loud.

"Dear Folks, I hope you are well. Here are some presents for the children. I hope they like them.

Your Loving Uncle Tom."

Daniel opened his box and looked inside. He whistled. "Brilliant." He put his hands in and brought out a beautiful black and green skateboard with purple wheels.

"It's perfect!" He watched as Henrietta opened her box. "I bet your present isn't as good as mine, Henrietta!"

Henrietta stuck out her tongue at Daniel and then watched as Dad opened the box addressed to Baby-Rose.

It contained a little pink duck on wheels, that made a QUACKING noise

when it was pulled along.

Baby-Rose began to drag it noisily across the floor of the kitchen.

"Right," shouted Henrietta, "now it's my turn." She turned her box upside down and shook it.

"Yippee!" she shrieked, as a pair of blue roller-skates crashed onto the floor and shot under the table. "They must be

the fastest roller-skates in the whole
world!"

"They won't be any use to you then,
will they!" sneered Daniel.

Henrietta narrowed her eyes. "Why
not?"

"Because you're the slowest roller-
skater in the whole world. A snail could
go faster than you, that's why!"

Henrietta frowned and clenched her fists.

"What did you say?"

Mum stood up and began clearing the table.

"Come on, you two. Don't start arguing this early in the morning. I'm not in the mood for it."

Dad held up the brown paper that had been wrapped around the parcel. "I've never seen a stamp like this before. Do either of you two want to keep it?"

Henrietta and Daniel both nodded their heads. "Yes please," they shouted together.

Dad laughed. "Well you'll have to share it then, won't you!" They both began to moan at once.

Dad sighed, then sat down and gave his usual lecture on the merits of sharing.

"It's not fair!" grumbled Henrietta. "I saw it first."

Daniel snorted. "Well I carried the parcel in so I should have it."

Dad groaned. "We'll sort it out later, but now you can both go upstairs and clean your teeth. Go on."

*　　*　　*

In the bathroom Henrietta put toothpaste on her brush and looked at Daniel out of the corner of her eye.

"Do you really want that stamp?"

Daniel nodded.

"So do I," Henrietta confided, "but we can't really share it, can we?" Daniel shook his head. He couldn't talk because he had a toothbrush in his mouth.

"I've got an idea," said Henrietta. "Why don't we have a race. You on your skateboard and me on my roller-skates. The winner gets to keep the stamp. Are you up for that?"

Daniel nodded and took the toothbrush

out of his mouth. "I'll win easily. You're useless on roller-skates."

Henrietta smiled one of her mysterious smiles.

"Maybe. Anyway, let's shake on it." They solemnly shook hands then Daniel wiped his mouth and went downstairs.

"You're going to lose this race," he shouted, "and the stamp!"

"That's what you think," whispered Henrietta. "But you're wrong, because I've got a plan! Hehehe."

She dried her hands. "Now where does Mum keep her superglue, I wonder?"

*   *   *

Five minutes later, outside the front of the house, Henrietta and Daniel were standing side by side on the pavement. Henrietta had strapped on her new roller-skates and Daniel was standing with one foot on his new black and green skateboard.

"Where shall we race to?" asked
Daniel.

Henrietta thought for a moment and
then pointed to a post box at the corner of
the street.

"From here to that post box. Are you
ready?"

Daniel nodded.

"Steady."

Daniel took his foot off the skateboard and said in his sensible adult-voice, "Are you sure you want to have this race, Henrietta? I'm bound to beat you. It doesn't seem fair, it's as if I'm stealing that stamp off you."

Henrietta grinned, "We'll see. Now where was I? Oh yes . . . GO!"

Daniel put one foot back on his skateboard and began pushing himself along with the other as fast as he could. "This is easy," he cried, as he raced along the pavement. "Come on, Henrietta, hurry up." He blinked. "What are you doing?"

For Henrietta had not moved a muscle. She looked as if she could not believe her eyes.

"What went wrong?" she cried. "I covered those wheels with superglue.

That skateboard should be stuck solid!"

She reached into her pocket, pulled out a small bottle and rubbed the dust off the label.

"Ratburgers," she groaned, "this isn't superglue. It's suntan lotion!"

"Come on," shouted Daniel, "I've

almost reached the post box." He looked back at Henrietta and laughed, "I told you I would win."

At that moment Henrietta wrinkled her nose. "I think some of that dust has gone up my, ah . . . my, ah . . . Oh no! Not my sneezy nose."

She turned round and tried to ignore it, but it wouldn't go away.

"ATISHOO!" She did a Henrietta hyper-sneeze that blew her along backwards on her roller-skates faster and faster until with a yell of "Yippee!" she shot past Daniel just in front of the post box.

"The winner is ME!" she cried, "so the stamp is mine. All MINE." She threw her arms into the air and began to dance around the lamp-post as Daniel slowly got off his skateboard.

He shook his head. "That was amazing, Henrietta. You were going backwards!

I've never seen anyone roller-skate
backwards that fast. How do you do it?"

Henrietta smiled. "It's easy. You just
have to follow your nose!" She giggled.
"Especially when it does a hyper-sneeze.
Hehehe."

STORY FOUR

THE FANCY DRESS PARTY

Henrietta sat up in bed and stretched out her arms.

"I wonder what time it is?" she yawned. She looked at the clock. "Ratburgers! It's far too early to wake up on a Saturday. I'm going back to sleep."

She lay down and pulled the covers over her head.

Suddenly she jumped up and clapped her hands.

"Yippee, I've just remembered. It's

Lucy's fancy dress party today." She began to sing at the top of her voice.

Her sensible brother Daniel poked his head round the door and groaned.

"Do you have to sing? It sounds awful at this time of the morning." He shook his head. "What am I saying? Your singing

sound awful at any time of the day at all!"

Henrietta stopped singing and leapt off the bed.

"It's Lucy's fancy dress party today," she cried, "and I'm going to win the prize for the best costume."

She skipped across the landing to the bathroom.

Daniel frowned. "How do you know you're going to win?"

Henrietta grinned. "Because I've just had a brilliant idea. Can I borrow your policeman's outfit?"

Daniel snorted.

"You can't go dressed as a policeman, you're a girl."

Henrietta sighed. "I know. That's why I shall go dressed as a policewoman. They wear almost the same clothes as policemen. I saw one yesterday wearing trousers so all I'll need is a hat."

Daniel shrugged his shoulders. "Please

yourself. You can borrow my costume if you want to. But if you ask me, I think you should go as a clown. Then you wouldn't have to dress up at all, you could just go as yourself."

He doubled up laughing at his own joke.

"I think you're going to look pretty stupid dressed as a policeman, Henrietta."

Henrietta turned and smiled her sweetest smile.

"Pretty, yes. Stupid, no. I leave that to you, Daniel. It's what you're best at!"

Before Daniel could reply, Henrietta had reached the bathroom, slammed the door in his face, and was singing to herself in the shower.

Daniel groaned and covered his ears as he ran downstairs.

"I know what I need," he muttered. "A

pair of earmuffs. Then I wouldn't have to listen to this racket every morning."

*   *   *

After breakfast Henrietta borrowed Daniel's policeman outfit and went up to her room to get ready. She stayed there all morning.

At lunchtime, she talked about nothing else but the party. She was so excited she only had *two* helpings of pudding.

After she had finished eating, she went straight back upstairs to her room.

"Mum!" she shouted, hours later. "What time do we have to leave for the party?"

"In five minutes! Have you finished getting that costume ready yet?"

"Nearly."

"Well, if you don't hurry up you'll be late. Then you'll never win that prize." There was a pause as Henrietta ran down the stairs.

"Mum, can you come and help me? I don't know which hat to wear. Please, Mum, please!" She smiled sweetly and flashed her eyelashes.

Her mother put down her knitting and shook her head. "I might have known." She sighed. "All right, I'll help you. We'd better hurry, though. We haven't got much time. Come on."

She picked up Baby-Rose, who was drawing a picture, and followed Henrietta up to her room.

*   *   *

"Do I look like a real policewoman?" asked Henrietta when her father opened the door two minutes later. He walked all round her and then nodded.

"Yes. You do. Except for one thing."

"What?"

"You aren't old enough to be a real policewoman."

He laughed.

Henrietta smiled.

"Seriously, Dad. Does the hat look OK? It's one of Mum's. I really want to win that prize." Her father nodded.

"The hat looks perfect and so do you."

Daniel popped his head round the
door.

"You'll be late for the party."

He looked at Henrietta's costume and
grinned.

"I said you would look stupid, and you
do. You'll never win that prize."

His father frowned. "If you're going to

be like that, Daniel, you can go straight to your room. Henrietta has worked very hard on that costume. The last thing she needs is you undermining her confidence."

Daniel shrugged.

"I still say she should go as a clown, she looks silly enough."

Henrietta squawked. "No I don't. Do I?"

She ran across the room and stared at herself in the mirror.

"He's right, I do look silly. I'll never win that prize." She sat down on the floor next to Baby-Rose and looked as if she was about to cry.

Baby-Rose laughed and tried to draw a big red dot on Henrietta's nose.

"It's not funny," groaned Henrietta as Baby-Rose tickled her nose with her pen. She stopped.

"Ah . . . ah . . . Oh no, not my sneezy nose." She reached for a hanky. But it was too late.

"ATISHOO!" She did a Henrietta hyper-sneeze that blew her right across the floor.

"Hahaha," laughed Daniel. "What do you look like?"

For when the hyper-sneeze had blown Henrietta across the floor it had also ripped a hole in her policewoman's trousers and made her policewoman's tie roll up into a ball.

As for the shoes, they were ruined. Their tops had been blown clean off.

But the worst thing, was Henrietta's poor nose. It was covered in red ink from Baby-Rose's pen.

"Now what do I do?" wailed Henrietta.

"Well it's too late to get changed," said her mother. "We're late already. You'll just have to go as you are and explain to Lucy what happened."

*   *   *

When Henrietta came back she burst into Daniel's room without knocking and leapt onto the bed. Daniel was deep into yet another new program on his computer. He looked up.

"Well, did they all laugh at you?"

"No," cried Henrietta. "I did what you said, and it worked. I told Lucy I was dressed as a clown and everyone agreed that I was the best clown they had ever

seen. So I won. Yippee!"

Henrietta began to bounce up and
down on Daniel's bed. As she bounced
she sang to herself at the top of her voice.

"What was the prize?" shouted Daniel,
covering his ears.

Henrietta stopped singing and
bouncing.

"I'm glad you asked me that, Daniel,
because I was thinking of giving you the
prize actually. It was your costume and
your idea that made me win after all."

Daniel smiled.

"Thanks, Henrietta. That's very kind of you."

Henrietta giggled.

"No it's not. Because the prize is a load of rubbish. Here, catch." She threw something onto Daniel's lap and began to bounce up and down on the bed once more.

"EARMUFFS!" cried Daniel. "You won a pair of earmuffs." He put them on as Henrietta began to sing one of her favourite songs.

He sighed. "They're not rubbish, Henrietta, they're perfect. Now I won't have to listen to your awful singing. Aaaah."

But Henrietta didn't hear him. She was too busy singing, as usual!

HENRIETTA AND THE TOOTH FAIRY

Stan Cullimore

Illustrated by John Farman

"Oh no. Not my sneezy nose." Henrietta tried to stop it. But it was too late . . .

Henrietta is always being naughty. She doesn't *want* to be like her sensible brother Daniel. And her sneezy nose keeps making her sneeze at all the wrong moments – at the swimming pool, buying new shoes, or trying to do good deeds. When Henrietta gets a wobbly tooth, she wants it to fall out quickly so that the tooth fairy will come. But things don't work out quite as Henrietta plans . . .

A delightful series of four stories about the mischievous Henrietta and her family – ideal for beginner readers.

'Children responded well to this lively, active book which has plenty of drawings to sustain their interest' *Federation of Children's Book Groups, Pick of the Year*

0 552 52745 9

YOUNG CORGI BOOKS

A LIST OF SELECTED TITLES
AVAILABLE FROM YOUNG CORGI

THE PRICES SHOWN BELOW WERE CORRECT AT THE TIME OF
GOING TO PRESS. HOWEVER TRANSWORLD PUBLISHERS
RESERVE THE RIGHT TO SHOW NEW RETAIL PRICES ON COVERS
WHICH MAY DIFFER FROM THOSE PREVIOUSLY ADVERTISED IN
THE TEXT OR ELSEWHERE.

All Young Corgi Books are available at your bookshop or newsagent, or can be
ordered from the following address:
Transworld Publishers Ltd,
Cash Sales Department,
PO Box 11, Falmouth, Cornwall TR10 9EN

Please send a cheque or postal order (no currency) and allow £1.00 for postage
and packing for one book, an additional 50p for a second book, and an additional
30p for each subsequent book ordered to a maximum charge of £3.00 if ordering
seven or more books.

Overseas customers, including Eire, please allow £2.00 for postage and packing
for the first book, an additional £1.00 for a second book, and an additional 50p
for each subsequent title ordered.

NAME (Block Letters) ....

ADDRESS ....

....